Lily Won't Sleep

Written by Alison Reynolds
Illustrations by Gail Yerrill

It was almost bedtime, but Lily did not want to go to sleep.

She was sure that there were monsters with spaghetti hair hiding in the darkness under her bed.

Lily put on her pyjamas very slowly.

She cleaned her teeth until they glistened and gleamed.

"It's time for bed," said Mum.
"I don't want to go to bed tonight," said Lily.

"But you're tired," said Mum.
"Lilys are NEVER tired!" shouted Lily ...

... and she ran downstairs.

Dad was eating a bowl of yellow jelly.
He gave Lily a spoon.

The jelly tasted yummy but the spoon grew heavier and heavier.
Lily's head started to nod up and down ...

"Lily you are really tired. Time for bed!" said Dad, wiping Lily's mouth.
"Lilys are NEVER tired!" shouted Lily, as she ran into the living room.

Lily curled up on the couch.
Mum gave her a cup of warm
milk to drink.

It was nice and cosy next to Mum.
Lily's eyes flicked open and closed ...

"Are you tired now?" said Mum, wiping Lily's chin.
"Lilys are NEVER tired!" shouted Lily.

"Little bear, are you frightened of going to bed?" asked Mum.

Lily nodded.

"There are monsters with spaghetti hair under my bed," she said.

"What? Monsters aren't allowed in here!" said Mum.

Mum and Dad marched up the stairs.
Lily tiptoed slowly up the stairs behind them.

"Strictly no monsters allowed in this house," said Dad loudly,
as he knocked on the bedroom door.

Mum flung open the door. She stomped into the bedroom and glared under the bed.

"Monsters with spaghetti hair go home!" she said.
"This is Lily's room."

Lily yawned and climbed into bed.

Dad turned off the big light and Mum turned on the nightlight.
"Thank you for chasing the monsters with spaghetti hair away," smiled Lily.

"Maybe this Lily is just a little bit tired,"
she whispered. "Goodnight."